DEVELOPING READER • 250-750 WORDS LEVEL 2

Penguin's Skating Party

by Dana Regan

SCHOLASTIC INC.

New York   Toronto   London   Auckland   Sydney
Mexico City   New Delhi   Hong Kong   Buenos Aires

The sun was out. The sky was blue.

It was a cold, cold day.

My friends came running to my house.

They shouted all the way.

"Hurry up!" said Penny.

"Put on your skates," said Pat.

"Today is Paula's birthday!"

I said, "Oh no! Not that."

"We're going to a party.
We'll meet behind the school.
We'll skate and spin and skate some more.
Doesn't that sound cool?"

They all were so excited. But I was feeling blue.
I had a great big secret. No one ever knew.

"I can't go," I sadly said.

"Why not?" asked Pat and Paul.

"It's no big deal," I said to them.

"I just can't skate. That's all."

"WHAT?" said Penny, Paul, and Pat.
"We all know how to skate!"
"I never learned," I had to say.
Pat said, "It's not too late!"

"Hurry up and get your skates.
Grab a hat. Let's go!
We are here to teach you
all that you need to know."

"First we need to show you
how to stand and how to glide.
Use your arms to help you.
We'll be right here by your side."

"Now, slowly bend your knees.
Now slowly move your feet.
That's good! Hooray! You did it!
You can skate!" said Pete.

"Now try it by yourself.
Arms out and lift your head.
Slide each skate a little bit.
You sure learn fast!" Pat said.

"I think I need to practice,"
I said to Penny, Pete, Paul, and Pat.
But the party was beginning.
There was no time for that.

We went to Paula's party. But I was still afraid.
I sat beside the snowbank and
that's where I would have stayed.

But Pete said, "Come and join us!
We're going to play a game.
It's crack the whip!" he said to me.
I didn't like that name.

Pat and I joined the line of
skaters as they passed.
I held on tight. I closed my eyes.
We were going very fast!

Then Pat let go. I slid by.
I began to spin around.
Everything sped past me from the
sky down to the ground.

I landed in the snowbank,
in a fluffy pile of snow.
My friends all skated to me.
They shouted, "Way to go!"

"That was the coolest crack the whip!
You skate just like a pro!"
They helped me up. And then I said,
"We'll skate some more. Let's go!"

Now I love to skate and spin.

I twirl and glide and play.

That party sure was lots of fun!

What a silly skating day!

To Joe and Tommy,
my favorite skating partners
—D.R.

No part of this publication may be reproduced, stored in a retrieval system, or transmitted in any form or by any means, electronic, mechanical, photocopying, recording, or otherwise, without written permission of the publisher. For information regarding permission, write to Scholastic Inc., Attention: Permissions Department, 557 Broadway, New York, NY 10012.

ISBN-13: 978-0-545-07080-5
ISBN-10: 0-545-07080-5

Text and illustrations copyright © 2009 by Dana Regan
All rights reserved. Published by Scholastic Inc.

SCHOLASTIC and associated logos are trademarks
and/or registered trademarks of Scholastic Inc.

Lexile is a registered trademark of MetaMetrics, Inc.

12 11 10 9 8 7 6 5 4 3 2 1   9 10 11 12 13 14/0

Printed in the U.S.A.
First printing, January 2009

Dear Family and Friends of New Readers,

Welcome to Scholastic Reader. We have taken more than eighty years of experience with teachers, parents, and children and put it into a program that is designed to match your child's interest and skills. Each Scholastic Reader is designed to support your child's efforts to learn how to read at every age and every stage.

- First Reader
- Preschool - Kindergarten
- ABC's
- First words

- Beginning Reader
- Preschool - Grade 1
- Sight words
- Words to sound out
- Simple sentences

- Developing Reader
- Grades 1 – 2
- New vocabulary
- Longer sentences

- Growing Reader
- Grades 1 – 3
- Reading for inspiration and information

On the back of every book, we have indicated the grade level, guided reading level, Lexile® level, and word count. You can use this information to find a book that is a good fit for your child.

For ideas about sharing books with your new reader, please visit www.scholastic.com. Enjoy helping your child learn to read and love to read!

Happy Reading!

—Francie Alexander
Chief Academic Officer
Scholastic Inc.